Water pure air so clean
Is a vision I have seen
And I know I'm not alone
We can find a way . . .

The audience was stunned into silence. It was Toby's song they heard, but it was their song, too — every song they had ever heard, every emotion they had ever felt. Helplessly they listened as Toby sang — each note reaching deeper into the forgotten hollows of their inner selves:

Humankind learn to share
Music is our only prayer . . .

Then the Dream Eater screamed, and hurled a barrage of images more terrifying than Toby had ever imagined, even in his wildest dreams. Giant squid wrapped tentacles around him. Monstrous seahawks swooped down, claws slashing. Nine-headed snakes boiled the water with their acrid breath, fangs spewing venom. "Surrender!"

"I'll never surrender to you," answered Toby, and sang:

Troubled seas, troubled land
One last chance to take a stand
And I know I'm not alone
We will find a way . . .

R. L. FISHER

THE PRINCE OF WHALES

TOR

A TOM DOHERTY ASSOCIATES BOOK

THE PRINCE OF WHALES

Copyright © 1985 by R. L. Fisher

Reprinted by arrangement with Carroll & Graf Publishers, Inc. and Quicksilver Books, Inc.

First Tor printing: October 1987

A TOR Book

Published by Tom Doherty Associates, Inc.
49 West 24 Street
New York, N.Y. 10010

ISBN: 0-812-56635-1
CAN. ED.: 0-812-56636-X

Printed in the United States of America

0 9 8 7 6 5 4 3 2 1

For you whose voice has yet to be heard,
whose song has yet to be sung . . .
Dream on!

PART
ONE

PART
ONE

1

In the waters of Arctic Bay a young whale sleeps. Others are not so lucky. . . .

"Toby, wake up."

The voice came from a distant place.

"Wake up," it said again.

Toby took no notice. He had music on his mind.

A louder, less gentle voice growled, "Cool it, you're makin' waves," in a low-pitched tone.

Thousands had come to the depths of Toby's dream, life in many forms from high and low, near and far. Tonight he was singing as never before. He could allow nothing to disturb him.

"Noise pollution," moaned a voice.

"Can't a whale get a little sleep around this place?" groaned another.

Toby answered with a stream of notes that began at the top of his range and cascaded effortlessly down to the bottom. The young dream singer would listen to no voice but his own.

Others tried in vain to stop the flow: "Quiet please!" "Cease!" "Desist!" "Abdicate!"

Toby tried to ignore the voices, but just as he reached the passage requiring his sharpest musical focus, the meddlesome hecklers shouted: "PIPE DOWN!" "NO MORE NOISE!" "WAKE UP AND SHUT UP!"

Concentration broken, Toby ended abruptly on an angry note that shook the sea. It was an act he instantly regretted. He had taken his listeners on a musical voyage and left them floundering in troubled waters.

Struggling to stay asleep, he apologized: "Forgive me."

The sea of faces began to fade and swirl.

"I must go now."

Then a force stronger than his own will swept Toby away.

"Wha ... What is it?" he sputtered, confused by the rude awakening. He opened one eye and moonlight rushed in.

"You've had another singing dream, Toby."

His other eye opened to the see the silhouette of his mother, Luma, floating graceful and immense in the dark water beside him.

"Did I wake the pod again?" Toby knew the answer. His dream songs always woke the others.

"Yes, you did," Luma replied sleepily.

"And did I make waves?" he asked, confirming what he already knew.

"Singing and making waves again."

"In my dream I was singing for an audience of thousands. . . ."

"It must have been wonderful." Luma yawned. "But not in the middle of the night." She rocked gently, nestling into the water. "Now go back to sleep and try not to dream too loudly."

Toby closed his eyes. Moments later he had drifted back to the Sea of Dreams.

2

The next day concern overflowed.

"Toby, it's time we had a little talk."

Before Brujon had said a word, Toby knew, just by looking at his father's haggard face and tired eyes, what the subject of this morning's discussion would be.

"I'm sorry Father. I can't help it. It just . . . happens."

"We understand that, Toby," said Brujon sternly, "but those infernal night sounds of yours are making nervous wrecks of us all. Complaints are pouring in from as far away as Baymouth. I don't have to remind you any sound that travels that far could attract the Beasts."

Luma had not missed a word. She too had heard the complaints and suffered the family's shame. Brujon's huge lower jaw was set firm, a sure indication of the stress he had been under. Concerned, she swam up next to them.

"What's all the foam and froth about?" she asked, quoting an old whale phrase. "We're safe here in Arctic Bay. And after all, it's not Toby's intention to bring the Iron Beasts down on us. He just happens to sing in his sleep. Is that such a terrible crime?"

Brujon raised his head above water to scan the bay.

"It may be more of a crime than we had ever imagined. You both know the importance of silence once the long swim south begins. We become prey for the Iron Beasts the moment we leave Arctic Bay. Some of our pod fear that Toby's night sounds will attract danger. Rumors are floating that Grampus is gathering support for a motion that would bring Toby before the Grand Council of Elders."

Luma's motherly concern quickly gave way to anger.

"The Grand Council!"

"Calm down, Luma." Brujon was anything but calm. "The others will hear."

"Let them! Just who does that Grampus think he is? An old fool! That's what! A dangerous old fool!"

Her voice boomed across the bay.

"Grampus is not the only one who feels that stern measures must be taken," said Brujon, trying to control his rising sense of frustration.

"You bet he's not the only one," Luma retorted. "I'll take stern measures with anyone who tries to drag our Toby's name through the mud. They'll get a sound piece of my mind and a good slap of my tail, too, if they refuse to listen to reason!"

"Grampus and the others make judgments only by what they hear," said Brujon. "You have to admit, Luma, that noise you so kindly refer to as singing is more than a little peculiar. I've never heard the like of it . Why . . . it's downright unwhalelike!"

"Unwhalelike!" Luma was livid. "Any sound Toby makes is whalelike. After all, he is a Great Winged Angel, just like you, me, and all the rest of us."

"Hrmph! That's not the point!" Brujon snorted. "The point is, anyone within a hundred miles could hear that noise on open sea. The Beasts have ears, too. And good ones! Our podmates are afraid, Luma. Afraid for their lives. And I can't really blame them. The way things are today, it's hard not to be afraid."

Luma nearly shouted: "You're defending them!"

Toby could hold silence no longer.

"But I can't help thinking that my dreams are trying to tell me something. Aunt Undeen told me . . ."

"Told you what?" Brujon interrupted. "That dream singers were once thought to be able to speak with spirits and do all kinds of miraculous things? That's just an old whale's tale, Toby. Even if it were true, do you think the others would believe us if we told them that our son is a dream singer with some kind of special mystical powers? You know as well as I do they'd think we were completely off the waves."

"If anyone's off the waves, it's that old barnacle-brain Grampus!" Luma exploded.

"Please don't argue anymore," Toby begged them. Never before had he heard such an outburst from his parents.

Brujon looked at his son and heaved a deep sigh of sympathy. Then he turned to Luma. "Toby's right. Arguing will get us nowhere. Let's put our heads together. Maybe we can resolve this problem once and for all."

After a long silence Luma's eyes brightened with the light of a memory remembered.

"I have an idea: Singing lessons! It came to me last night as I was dozing off for the second, or was it the third, time? I had forgotten it until this very moment. Toby's dream music only comes out at night when everyone is trying to sleep. If those musical impulses could be transferred to daylight, there would be far less cause for complaint. I understand that Maestro Baleeni might be accepting a few new students. Perhaps we should speak with him."

Brujon pondered. "Singing lessons . . ."

Luma's idea could not have been worse as far as Toby was concerned. Maestro Baleeni was flippers and fins the finest singer in Arctic Bay, but as a teacher he had the reputation of being a musical stickler for whom even technical perfection was not enough. The situation being what it was, Toby decided not to voice his objections. It would be best to keep his big mouth shut.

For the first time that morning a smile crept across Brujon's face.

"You know, Luma," he said at last, "you may have something there. That old taskmaster Baleeni could be just what Toby needs."

3

The audition began on a loud note.

Maestro Baleeni took one look at Toby and started to laugh. His resounding basso profundo bellowed like short bursts of a foghorn.

"So!" he declared. "You are the creator of those remarkable sounds!"

The maestro began to say something else, but his words were stifled by another round of wave-shaking laughter.

"Forgive me, Toby." Maestro Baleeni struggled to keep a straight face. "I know we have serious business to attend to." The maestro's massive belly started to shake again, causing great waves in the caverns that served as the singing school, and the only words he managed to say before resuming his laughter were: "But first I must have a good laugh!"

The outburst that followed ricocheted around the caverns like a hundred foghorns gone berserk.

Toby liked a good joke as well as the next whale, but the humor of this one escaped him. This was not at all what he had expected. Maestro Baleeni was supposed to be a serious musician. If first impressions were to be believed, the jovial singing master was some kind of raving lunatic.

"I'm sorry," he said at last. "You must think me very rude, but I was laughing with you, not at you. You see, when I was a young whale, I too made strange sounds in my sleep. But I never caused such a stir! My father, bless his dear departed soul, would not allow it."

Maestro Baleeni's face was transformed by a look of pain mixed with pleasure as he remembered a time long ago.

"You see, my father lived through the darkest age of Great Winged Angel history, the era when our numbers had dwindled to near extinction. When no singing was allowed, none at all. That is why he was undoubtedly one of the worst singers who ever lived. At first hint of one of my midnight rhapsodies he would moon so loudly in my ear and so dreadfully off-key that I had no choice but to wake up. When I hear your nightly noises, Toby,

I am reminded of my father when he sang so badly in my ear!"

Once again the cavernous halls of the singing school shook with the maestro's laughter. This time the laughter was contagious and, in spite of himself, Toby started to laugh. Then, as if by signal, Maestro Baleeni's smile faded. His eyes narrowed and took on a peculiar and very serious glint.

Toby's first lesson was about to begin.

"Building song castles in the night sea and singing are two very different things." Maestro Baleeni spoke in a deep, somber voice. "A singer must know scales, arpeggios, tone production, rhythm, melody, and harmony. He must be able to distinguish in-tune from out-of-tune and good music from bad. He must have the patience of an oyster, the logic of a crab, and the soul of an angelfish. In short, he must be a master of music and a master of himself."

Maestro Baleeni paused to let his words sink in.

"Music, my young hopeful, is both an art and a science. To achieve a balanced blend of these two elements requires years of study and discipline and a special something else. Some call it talent, but I choose to call it courage. The courage to be yourself. Before you can express your feelings, you must know what your feelings are, where they come from. The path of music is not for those who are weak at heart. Few today are willing to endure the hardships."

A faraway look came to the maestro's eyes and a furrow creased his weathered brow.

"It was not always so. At one time there were many great singers and great audiences to appreciate them. When a concert was given, there was magic in the sea. Our voices carried music halfway around the world. Music was no mere entertainment in those days. It was our language, our history, the very soul of our culture. So important was the role of music in our ancestors' lives that in the seven main music-language systems, of which there were hundreds of offshoots, there was no single word for music, the closest being the word for life itself."

The maestro spouted a plume of vapor from his air hole.

"That was before the humans invented the exploding harpoon. Before great Iron Beasts hunted and slaughtered us. Before mammoth tankers spilled foul, black scum into our waters and drowned out our voices with the constant rumble of their churning fins."

Toby listened, transfixed by the maestro's words.

"A new mood has befallen us, Toby, a mood of fear, suspicion, and confusion. Imagine! Great Winged Angels, Nature's most majestic breed, once the greatest singers in all the seas, hunted like animals! Afraid to sing for fear the Iron Beasts will hear us. It used to be that everyone sang. Today it is only the few remaining singers who sing, and only in summer, and only in the safety of the bays. It's a terrible situation, terrible indeed. The old ways have little meaning for us today. The great singers died, and with each death another song was gone." The maestro spoke slowly, deliberately, each word coming from the depths of his being.

"No, Toby, nothing is as it was."

The good maestro seemed lost in another time and place. Then, remembering Toby's presence, he smiled and released a long breath. "I have talked long enough. Now let me hear you sing."

Stunned by the sudden shift, Toby stammered, "What . . . ah . . . do you want me to sing?"

"Anything," said the maestro, "anything at all. Don't be shy. Sing!"

"Er . . . well . . . I don't really know any songs all the way through. I just sing . . . ah . . . in my dreams."

"One of the traditional songs perhaps?"

Toby had heard the traditional songs many times, but he could not recall any of them.

"Never mind, my dear young dream singer. We will make up our own song. I will start. You follow."

Maestro Baleeni began to sing. Toby followed as best he could, but it was soon apparent that he was no match for the maestro whose voice was more powerful than ten steamships and more agile than a shoal of singing sea gazelles. They leapt from note to note, fast notes and slow, high notes and low, short notes, long notes, soft notes and loud. Then, as abruptly as it had begun, the lesson ended.

"I have heard enough!" The maestro's face might have been etched in stone but his eyes belied a less solemn intent. "I will teach you! Anyone with as big a reputation as you have, before learning one song, must surely be destined for greatness!"

There was another outburst of laughter from the maestro, whose only weakness seemed to be laughing at his own jokes.

Then he was serious again.

"I warn you that I do not waste my time on students who refuse to apply themselves. You must develop your natural abilities. It will take work, work, and more work. Come at the same time tomorrow and we will begin in earnest. I will teach you an ancient song of protection. Who knows? Perhaps it may be of use to you someday. When you have music, Toby, you are never alone."

Maestro Baleeni swam away, singing a beautiful melody that haunted Toby for hours to come. It would not be easy to live up to the master's high expectations. Yet the maestro had stirred something within him, a deep feeling that told him music was the answer to the mystery, the mystery of his dreams.

4

For a time the lessons worked wonders.

Two complete cycles of the moon had passed without a single dream song being heard. Maestro Baleeni's reputation had risen to almost heroic proportions. Brujon could not have been more pleased. Peaceful nights had once again returned to Arctic Bay.

Mastering the maestro's lessons was even more difficult than Toby had expected. The maestro was a singer of the old school—which meant that there was one way to sing his exercises, and one way only. Yet it was a labor of love, and Toby practiced with all-consuming passion.

If not complete acceptance, the pod seemed to at least be giving Toby the benefit of the doubt. Even Serena, the Great Winged Angel of his dreams, had seen fit to smile at him once when their paths happened to cross not so long ago. That in itself would have been cause for celebration, but combined with his whale-sized appetite for day music and the other blessings that were flowing his way, it seemed that Toby's life had taken a distinct turn for the better. In fact, he could not remember a happier time.

Then, one night when it was least expected, music spilled back into Toby's dreams. It was soft and almost sweet at first, and easily forgiven, but it grew louder and stronger until all of the whales had been awakened. The dream songs had returned. There was panic in the pod!

Early the next morning a formal complaint was lodged with the Grand Council of Elders. The sun had not reached mid-position in the sky when crotchety old Grampus swam up to Brujon and officiously announced:

"It is my duty to inform you that the Grand Council of Elders requests ... er ... rather, it commands your presence three days hence at a hearing to determine the fate of your son, a certain Toby Whale. The charge: Endangering the Pod!"

Luma and Brujon's worst fears were confirmed. Endangering the Pod carried a maximum sentence of banishment. They knew that a young whale as trusting and impressionable as Toby would not stand a chance alone on open sea. He would surely be savaged by the crushing jaws of sharks, the razor teeth of killer whales, or the deadly exploding spears of the great Iron Beasts.

The dreaded day of Toby's trial arrived all too soon. The seven elders listened as the testimony for both sides was presented.

Grampus, the instigator of the complaint, argued convincingly:

"More than the loss of sleep is at stake here. Those night sounds pose a serious threat to our security. I say we banish the young noisemaker now or risk the wrath of the Beasts!"

Luma, then Brujon, pleaded in their son's behalf:

"Toby means no harm. He is not even aware of his actions. Banishment is much too serious a sentence for an unconscious act such as singing in one's sleep.

"He has never been in trouble before. We beg the learned Council to have mercy."

In an impassioned speech Maestro Baleeni appealed for clemency:

"If not the most accomplished of my students, Toby is certainly the most highly motivated. As a teacher, musician, and citizen of the sea, I implore you: Do not condemn an innocent young whale who could one day enrich our lives with music. In these troubled times a young and healthy whale, especially one who could become a singer, is too precious a gift to waste!"

When all the testimony had been heard, the Grand Council of Elders retired to their submerged chambers where they would decide the fate of one Toby Whale.

The Grand Council deliberated for what seemed an eternity. Loud, muffled rumblings came from beneath the water. The Council was in heated debate. Pod members milled around, discussing the case in hushed tones. Except for an occasional sidelong glance in Toby's direction, it was as if he did not exist.

"Perhaps I have become invisible," thought Toby. "Maybe this is all just a bad dream. Thank the deep north waters Aunt Undeen is on the Council. At least *she* won't let me down."

There was a murmur of excitement. The Grand Council of Elders was returning. They looked irritable as they filed in, eyes fixed forward, saying nothing. Aunt Undeen was the last to emerge from chambers. Being the eldest member of the pod, Undeen was the Grand Elder of the Grand Council of Elders. It was she who spoke for them:

"This has been a most difficult case." Her wavering voice creaked and cracked under the weight of a hundred summers. "Unlike our relatives of toothed extraction—orcas, cachelots, and the like—we Great Winged Angels are a peace-loving breed. It would be unthinkable for us to commit a crime of a violent nature. The average case heard before this corpulent body might be one involving a whale who has spoken out of turn or merely hurt another whale's feelings. In cases such as these the disgrace of having to appear before the Grand Council of Elders is considered punishment enough and the defendant is released after receiving a stern but gentle admonition. A much more serious charge has been leveled against Toby Whale. Endangering the Pod, Toby's alleged offense, carries with it a maximum penalty of banishment, which is the most severe penalty the Grand Council can impose. Endangering the Pod is a *very* grave charge indeed."

"Get on with it," muttered a Council member under his breath.

That comment, in Undeen's younger days, would have provoked a comeback such as, "Watch your tongue, Blubberbreath!"

She was much too old to give a bubble about what anyone thought of her, and all those who knew her knew she'd not be rushed. As it was, like her other faculties, Undeen's hearing was not what it used to be. She missed the comment entirely and continued undaunted:

"The Council was deadlocked, three in favor of the maximum penalty, three opposed. Normally, in a case such as this, the Grand Elder—that's me—would cast the deciding vote. In this case, however, the fairness of the arbiter came into question. I am, you will remember, the defendant's great aunt, and as such I was, justly or unjustly, accused of family favoritism."

Undeen glared at the member of the Grand Council who was undoubtedly her accuser. Her palsied jowls shook, but only slightly, as she turned her attention back to the proceedings.

"Let's see ..." She paused while her memory struggled to catch up with her mouth. "Yes, now I remember. When the fairness of the arbiter comes into question, no verdict can be rendered and a curious and little known legal ordinance goes into effect. To wit: the defendant must decide his own fate.

"Toby Whale, it is my unhappy task to inform you that you have until the first day of migration to decide what your sentence, if any, shall be. And with that I hereby declare the case of Toby Whale ... ah ... open ... closed. Open and closed."

Everyone swam away bewildered, but none more so than Toby. What was he to do? One thing was certain. If he did not put an end to his dream songs before the long swim south began, he and his pod could be in deep trouble.

Night after night he urged his sleeping mind to be still.

"Please, my sleeping mind, do not sing tonight. Think of me. Think of the others. Think of the shame on my family's good name!"

Toby's pleadings meant nothing to his sleeping mind, and the shame on the family's name even less. And so it was that the harder he fought to stop his sleeping mind from singing, the louder and more frequent his dream songs became.

5

From a depth of nine fathoms Toby searched the surface for shrimp.

It was the last day before the long swim south would begin and his last chance at a decent meal. Food would be scarce until next spring, when the pod would return to the generous waters of Arctic Bay. The past weeks had brought no relief from the pressure. Toby's attempts to stop his dream songs had failed miserably and the complaints had become more bitter than ever. He had still not decided what, if any, his punishment would be.

A visit with his aunt Undeen brought no positive results.

"I sincerely wish I could help you, Toby," she said, "but an Order of Silence prevents me from discussing your case."

When he asked her about the dream singers of

olden times, she could only reply, "There was a legend. Something about a dream singer rising from the depths to restore the ancient wisdom." She paused for an endless moment. "Now what was it we were talking about?"

"Dream singers ... The legend ... Restoring the ancient wisdom ..."

"Oh, yes. There was a legend. I'm afraid it escapes me. The banks of my memory, Toby, have all but washed away."

That was yesterday. This morning Toby could worry about nothing but eating. Spotting a likely catch of krill-shrimp he spiraled upward, allowing air to escape from his back-mounted spout. Bubbles rose to the surface, forming a net around his intended meal. It was a standard technique that had earned him many delicious meals and there was no reason why it should not work again. All that was left to do was swim up through the center of the circle of bubbles and have lunch in one open-mouthed lunge.

Just as he was beginning the upward ascent, he noticed that Serena had taken a fishing position nearby. Toby and Serena had grown up together and before Toby's dreams had become a problem they had been closest of friends. Lately Serena had avoided him like a red tide. There was something different about her, something he could not explain. Drawn like a

magnet, his eyes followed her every move. The next thing he knew, the shrimp he had meant to catch had scattered.

Toby searched and spotted another cluster of shrimp. Circling upward, he began to blow a second bubble net. Everything was going smoothly until he happened to glance over at Serena, who was busy doing the same thing. Suddenly spellbound, Toby watched her rise in a natural sweeping motion and deftly capture a foamy mouthful. By the time his attention returned, Toby's intended catch had escaped again.

He was beginning to wonder if he would ever get his fill. Sighting a third drift of shrimp, he angled upward, stealthily stalking his prey. When he got within striking distance, he took aim and flicked his tail forward with a mighty thrust.

A cresting arc of spray flew upward over Toby's back and beyond the proposed catch, striking the surface with a loud splash. The shrimp, as expected, swam back towards him. This time it seemed he couldn't miss. But just then, from the corner of his eye, Toby caught another glimpse of Serena. There *was* something different about her. She was beautiful!

A wave of shrimp spilled over Toby's face. He had forgotten to open his mouth!

Embarrassed by his blunders, Toby vowed not to be so foolish again. He swam to the far side of Arctic Bay where his full attention could be given to catching shrimp. By nightfall he had satisfied his body's hunger, yet he still felt empty inside. A sad longing settled over him as he slowly swam back across the bay, a hurt that would not subside.

Serena, you are
As distant as yesterday,
Like light from a star,
So bright yet so far away.

How can you be so cold
To one who adores you,
Who'd love you for life
And never ignore you?

How can you be so cold to me?

6

The long swim south would begin at daybreak. Though eagerly looking forward to the change of seascape, Toby was afraid to go to sleep. It would not do to upset the pod on their last night in Arctic Bay.

The starry autumn sky made him wonder. "My dreams *must* be trying to tell me something. If only I knew what it was...."

Slowly Toby's imagination began to wander to far-off places. Thought fragments and scattered images mingled. Visions of sunsets on peaceful distant waters and slow-moving clouds rolled by on the back of his eyelids. Swaying sealife danced to the endless music of the waves. Finally he drifted into a soft, peaceful twilight sleep.

And when he was suspended in the space where imagination and reality meet, a stream of images, shapes, and colors flooded his senses with visions of the most wondrous kind. Feeling light, almost weightless, and enjoying the visions immensely, Toby did not notice at first that a sound had joined the flow—a high, grating squeal.

The sound and visions fused together, rising to a screaming fever pitch. Wide awake again and paralyzed by some unseen force, Toby struggled to break the grip of terror that was strangling him. Stiff with fear, he hung on for dear life while the sound and visions grew to hurricane force. Then, in a deafening explosion of sounds and terrifying visions, it ended.

The next thing he knew, Toby was floating in a quiet place that looked curiously familiar. Dazzling colors from the most subtle pastels to the most electric reds and yellows filled the surrounding sea and air. Looking up into the sky, he noticed that the moon and stars, though flashing like lighthouse beacons and changing colors in the manner of chameleon fish, were in their usual positions. It was then that he suddenly realized this was the same place he had been before the explosion. But how different it looked. How strangely enchanting . . .

A new light, like a flame with no center, bathed Toby in a soft, warm glow, and a feeling of deep relief and well-being came over him.

"Welcome to the other side."

Startled by the unfamiliar voice, Toby searched but could not pinpoint the source. It seemed to come from everywhere at once.

"Don't be alarmed," came the voice again, clear and compelling. "I should be visible to you any second now."

Toby had no chance to ponder the words. Suddenly the light became bright white and he was confronted by the abrupt appearance of a magnificent multicolored flying whale. The gigantic creature hovered above him, filling half the sky. So intense was its blazing glare that Toby had to squint just to look at it. Through eyes that were just slits he saw that the creature, though in whale form, was not at all a whale in the ordinary sense, but a shimmering apparition of iridescent lights and colors in constant motion.

"I'm sorry to make such a production of this," said the creature, "but becoming visible is something I so rarely do."

In a flash the enormous fiery finback shrank to the size of a small goldfish before Toby's astonished eyes.

"There, that's better. No need for big where small will do. Allow me to introduce myself. My name is a rather clumsy one, I'm afraid—Theophilous. I've been meaning to change it for the last few hundred years, but I just never seem to come up with one I like better. Anyway, my friends call me Thes. I hope, Toby, that you will do the same."

Toby was rightfully astounded, but more than a little unnerved by the fact that when Thes spoke his mouth did not seem to budge so much as a twitch.

"My mouth does not move because we spirits speak directly from mind to mind. We can speak without moving our lips, change shapes at will, and fly on the wings of song, but it is becoming very difficult for us to make the slightest stir in the physical world. Physical beings and spirits used to be much more in tune with one another and Nature always managed to keep herself on an even keel. Lately the dear old lady's been listing starboard. It's not her fault. The problem is that the human beings have lost their sense of balance, and if something is not done soon, they could destroy what has taken Nature millions of years to achieve. Nature's song, the sound of everything at once, is in danger of becoming so out of tune that it may soon become the sound of nothing at all."

The only humans Toby had encountered were boatloads of well-meaning whale watchers who were often a nuisance but never really dangerous.

"Among them are many loving souls," came Thes's

instant reply. "We just can't understand what's got into them. Little by little they seem to be drifting away from the lighter side of their nature to dwell in the denser plane. We've tried to reason with them. We've invaded their dreams. We've appeared to them in visions, but they refuse to change their wasteful ways. They've turned a deaf ear to us, Toby. We need your help to get the message across."

"How could I help?" Toby wondered.

"Your voice!" the spirit exclaimed. "Dream singers are as rare as clam's teeth these days!"

"Dream singers!" thought Toby. "Does that mean my dreams really do have a purpose?"

"Dreams are the seeds of ideas, Toby, but you must act upon them if they are ever to amount to anything. They're your inner strength. Your outer strength is how you use them."

"My aunt Undeen once told me that dream singers were thought to have some kind of special mystical powers."

Thes changed to a pale sky blue.

"I never thought of it in quite that way. . . ." Thes's thought waves seemed so distant that he might have been thinking only to himself. "But, yes, I suppose that by today's standards the powers of the dream singers *would* have to be considered both special and mystical."

Thes turned to gold, remembering.

"You see, Toby, back in the Golden Age of Great Winged Angel music, dream singing was not thought to be mystical in the least. It was a completely natural occurrence, as predictable as the next wave, as real as the mother sea herself."

"What exactly did the dream singers do?" Toby wondered.

"Even we spirits don't know the half of what they really did," Thes answered. "Publicly—in society—they functioned as seers, sorcerers, teachers, story-tellers. They were valued as keepers of history, esteemed as upholders of the ancient traditions. Yet there was another side to them. Their deepest secrets were shared by only a few. Wise elders, masters of dream music, could somehow interpret the songs of the dream singers to determine such matters as a change of fishing grounds or the choosing of a new migration route. Dream music contributed to every aspect of Great Winged Angel life."

"You said *I* was a dream singer," Toby reminded him.

"You are, Toby, but as far as I know, there is no one alive who can interpret your dream songs. Had you been born two or three hundred years ago, you would have apprenticed with a master singer. Then after years of study you would have left your pod on a song quest and not returned until you had found your real voice."

"Song quest?" thought Toby. "Real voice? I've never heard of such things."

"Dream singers, as part of their training to become master singers, would go out alone on open sea in search of a musical vision," Thes explained. "Of course, it was not nearly as dangerous then as it is today. When the dream singer had found the song that balanced heart and mind, it was said that he or she had found their real voice."

"A song quest," thought Toby. "Maybe that's what I should do."

"It is not something to be entered into lightly, Toby."

"But I've got to do something. The Grand Council of Elders gave me until tomorrow morning to decide my fate. I was charged with disturbing the pod."

"Yes, Toby, I know. I know all about that. Don't worry; the answer will come."

Thes chuckled, sending colorful waves of joy in all directions.

"Your aunt Undeen attended one of the last great musical feasts held in honor of a dream singer's emergence to songhood. It's no surprise that she does not remember. It happened close to a hundred years ago, when she was just a young whalechild. Of course, whales have always used practically any excuse to hold a feast, but this was a very special occasion. Pods came from miles around for twelve days of celebration. Marine life of all kinds joined in the festivities. Master singers competed to see who could project the most stunning and elaborate musical pictures into the air. So great were their powers that their songs could be seen with the eyes as well as heard with the ears. The feast celebrating the emergence to songhood was one of the most important events in the dream singer's life. It would still be years before they could truly be called master singers, but from the final day of the festivities until they died, the dream singers were venerated as living treasures."

Toby was lost in his imaginings for a long moment.

"My voice," he thought. "You said it could help you. How would that work?"

Thes clapped his little flippers together in front of him.

"Why, by singing, of course! Music is the multiversal language. The problem is we spirits don't have voices that human ears can hear. Our music goes right over their heads. They *could* hear us if they listened with their hearts, but they've forgotten how to listen with their hearts. If we can teach physical beings such as yourself to translate your music into a form that the humans can understand, we may be able to reach their hearts through their ears."

Toby's eyes blinked in bewilderment.

"It is most difficult to explain, Toby, but easy to demonstrate. The humans have a weakness for music. If you will allow me to borrow your voice for a little while, I will show you why that weakness must be exploited."

Under normal circumstances Toby would have been more than a little wary about lending his voice to a stranger, but already he sensed that Thes could be trusted. Besides, his curiosity was boundless.

"What do I have to do?"

"Just relax. Surrender to the sound," Thes replied. "No harm will come to you. Spirit music has a very powerful effect, so be prepared. The song of the spirit has wings."

7

Toby felt a warm tingle in the back of his brain.

A moment later he was engulfed by sounds like none he had ever heard, high and low, loud and soft, all at the same time. Imagine his astonishment when he realized that the strange music was coming from him!

The fact that Thes was using Toby's voice did not hinder his ability to transmit thoughts.

"Before we embark on our journey I should warn you of the hazards. Sound-wave travel is perfectly safe unless fear takes control. You must remain relaxed so that the sound, our source of energy, may continue. Should the sound stop, you could snap back into your physical body, making it most difficult for you to reach this side again. Don't worry; I will be with you."

Thes raised Toby's vocal vibrations to a higher pitch. The next thing Toby knew, he was hovering above the waves.

"Hold on," said Thes. "Here we go."

The vibrations increased again, and Toby felt himself rising, slowly at first, then faster and higher until his physical body was just a speck of gray matter in the water far below. Terror gripped Toby by the throat and started to squeeze. The sound stopped. Suddenly he began to fall.

"Relax," urged Thes. "Surrender to the song."

"I can't relax," thought Toby, as he whooshed through a flock of high flying birds. "If whales had been meant to fly, Great Blue would have given us wings."

"But you do have wings," insisted Thes, "your water wings. Use them!"

By extending his flippers, Toby quickly learned that he could swim in the air in the same way as he swam in the sea. The sound returned and he leveled off. It was not long before Toby was actually enjoying the sensation of fast flight.

In nearly no time he had seen more of the world than one is likely to see in a lifetime. His excited eyes had encountered every continent, ocean and mountain range, desert and jungle, and the vast expanses of ice at both poles.

They flew in darkness and in light, in desert heat and tropical humidity, in rain and hail and snow and sleet. Over mountains and fields and rocky shores. Through night and day three times and back again. And just when it seemed that Toby's eyes, his very senses, would explode from so much stimulation, they paused to hover above a gigantic, seemingly endless cloud of purple smoke.

"What is it?" Toby wondered.

"You have seen the world of nature," said Thes. "Now let me introduce you to the human world. The haze is smog, one of the many by-products of what the humans once called progress. A large city lies below."

The sound changed to a lower vibration and they descended through the chemical clouds. When Toby caught his first glimpse of the city, with its massive skyscrapers, bridges, and traffic jams, he suffered a shock of the first water. It was a frightening sight that made his eyes practically jump right from his head. Lights were flashing, horns blasting, cars, trucks, buses, rushing every which way. There was a riot in the streets!

As they hovered, Thes spoke directly into Toby's inner ears:

"Long ago the humans lived a simple life. They lived in harmony because they were in tune with

Nature's song. Then they invented money, machines, and their great god, Science. Now there is so much noise around that they can barely hear themselves think. They are causing so much static in the sound of everything at once that we spirits are having trouble keeping Nature's song in tune."

Thes increased the sonic vibrations and they flew above the city, pausing to examine both the beauty and the ugliness of the human creation. They saw museums, parks, art galleries and sporting events, prisons, factories, military bases and power plants. Their last stop was an outdoor concert where Toby heard what was, for him, a strange and totally mystifying cacophony, the sound of human music.

After one last look at the city they sailed back over the ocean on waves of sound.

"There is just one more thing I am afraid you must see," said Thes. "Be prepared; it will be a horrifying sight."

Moments later they glided down toward a ship of the kind that Toby had only heard of but never seen: a dreaded Iron Beast. A gagging stench rose up from it, and as Thes predicted, the sight was enough to make any whale cringe. The body of a whale was on the deck. Men with long flensing knives were cutting deep gouges into the still-living flesh.

"There is not a single product provided by whales

that the humans cannot make in other ways," Thes said grimly. "With great factory ships like these, whalemen can kill, skin, and process a whale in less time than you can hold your breath."

Toby was overcome by grief for his fellow beings who had met such a tragic fate. Anger welled inside him at the humans and what they had done. It was then he knew that he would do anything in his power to help end their mindless rampage against Nature.

"The humans can be very cruel, but hating them will do no good. We've got to reach them before they close themselves off altogether. Now we'd better be heading back. You have a long migration ahead and need all the rest you can get."

When they had arrived above Toby's sleeping body, they hovered while Thes placed some parting thoughts directly into Toby's eager, questioning mind:

"If all goes according to plan, we should be ready to launch a full-scale attack on human hearts before the vernal equinox. Listen with your inner ears. Tune into the sound of everything at once. And above all, don't fight your dreams. They are as much a part of you as swimming and catching shrimp. Accept them. Orchestrate them. Learn to direct that dream energy to places where it is needed. Remember these three things well, for they could mean the difference between life and death some day. They are the way to the real voice, and the real voice will be both your shield and your most powerful weapon when the true test comes."

"Do you really think I could help?" asked Toby.

"There are many brave hearts asleep on land and in the sea," Thes said. "We must find them and awaken them. Birds. Wolves. Elephants. Whales. Even some humans can still hear the sound of Nature's song. Sealife and wildlife from all over the world will sing together in a grand chorus. If that does not touch the hearts of the humans, nothing will. Until we meet again, Toby: Swim with the Spirit!"

The sound that had carried them abruptly stopped and Toby floated down, like a stray pelican's feather.

For what was left of the night, he slept a deep and dreamless sleep.

PART TWO

8

Morning came and Toby awoke refreshed. The calm waters of the bay glistened red and gold in the first rays of sunlight and the sky was clear except for a slight haze. A perfect day for his song quest to begin.

Memories flooded his senses. If anyone had tried to tell him as short a time ago as yesterday that there was another world as different as water is to air on the other side of this world, he would surely have scoffed and thought they had water on the brain. Yet he'd been there and seen it with his own eyes. It simply could not have been a dream.

He was aroused from his reverie by an age-old chant for togetherness that signaled the beginning of the migration ceremonies. No one seemed to know where or when the ritual had begun. According to Aunt Undeen, Great Blue, the mother of all whales, had originated the ceremonies before the dawn of whale history.

When the chants and prayers for a safe passage ended, Brujon had some stern advice for his son: "Toby, I don't have to remind you, but I will anyway. . . ."

"Father, I've decided. . ."

"The sea can be a dangerous place. Only the quick of wit and stout of heart survive."

"Father, it's just that . . ."

"So keep your wits about you, Son. Thank Great Blue you didn't sing in your sleep last night."

"Father?"

"Maybe you've finally got those dream songs under control. If you must sing while we are travelling . . ."

"Father!"

"What is it, Toby? I'm talking to you."

"There's something I have to tell you," said Toby. "I won't be traveling with the pod. I've decided to go on a song quest. I have to find my real voice."

Toby wanted desperately to tell of his adventure with Thes, but decided that this was neither the time nor the place. Brujon would think it was just another whalechild's fantasy.

"Luma, come quickly. Our son has lost his mind."

Luma swam swiftly toward them. "What wrong?" she asked.

"Toby says he won't be swimming with us. He has to go on a song quest to find his real voice."

"A song quest, Toby?"

"Didn't the dream singers used to do it?" asked Toby, hiding his sources.

"So!" shouted Brujon. "Your aunt Undeen has been filling your head with her silly ideas. Well, listen to me, young whale. What dream singers might or might not have done is no concern of yours."

"But I have to do something, Father. Even you said that my dream songs could attract the Iron Beasts."

"What if . . ." Luma's mind was churning. "What if Toby swam far enough away from the pod so as not to bother anyone, but never completely out of hearing range?"

Brujon thought for a long moment before he answered.

"That way he could call for help if he was ever in trouble."

"And everyone would be happy," Toby added.

"It's settled then," said Brujon. "Now don't forget what I told you, Toby: Stay away from black water, Son, and red tides. They're poison, pure poison. . . ."

And so it was agreed. They said their good-byes. Luma cried, but only a little. Brujon offered no end of sound advice. And as the pod departed from Arctic

Bay, traveling due south, Toby set out on his own, following a parallel route. His first moments alone were filled with apprehension. The pod had just disappeared over the horizon when his nerves started to twitch and little doubts began to seep into the network of crevices at the fringes of his mind. Didn't Thes say that a song quest should not be entered into lightly? Did he not imply that it could be very dangerous?

The song quest had begun.

9

For the first time in his life Toby was truly a whale with a purpose. Finding his real voice was his goal, and swimming apart from the pod, he was free to sing to his heart's content.

By listening closely to his inner ears, Toby discovered he could hear the sound of everything at once. The wind, the waves, and the murmur of rising bubbles were all a part of Nature's song. Toby listened and learned. By the time a week had passed his memory banks were filled with new songs waiting to be released when the right time came.

Late one afternoon a school of friendly dolphins joined the pod. One of them, whose name was Chetly, heard singing in the distance and swam to investigate. At first Toby did not notice the dolphin's arrival. When he did look up, he was a little startled. The two exchanged nods and glances; then Chetly settled down, content to listen.

A short while later Chetly, who was no stranger to music, began to sing. The dolphin's music differed from Toby's in many ways. His voice was much higher pitched, and he had a curious way of phrasing, placing emphasis on odd parts of the rhythm. But the two styles blended in a harmonious way, and soon Toby and Chetly were singing as if they had sung together all their lives.

When the music reached the others, several took an interest and came to listen. Maestro Baleeni was the first to arrive. He had a puzzled expression at first, but it soon changed to a smile when he heard the astonishing improvement in Toby's voice.

"The young dolphin," he remarked to himself, "also has the makings of a fine singer."

Then the maestro added his voice to the song.

From the trio a small chorus grew. Chances to hear Baleeni sing were few and eagerly awaited. He sang above them and below them, weaving melodies and harmonies that seemed complicated but at the same time stunningly simple. That the maestro had mastered his craft was proved by every note he sang.

Soon others started singing and joyous music filled the sea until the sun was low in the sky. Then, regretfully, it was time to disband. As they exchanged farewells, Toby gave silent thanks to Great Blue or whoever had invented music. Happily lost in thought he did not notice when Serena swam up beside him.

"Your singing was beautiful today, Toby."

"Thank you," he said stiffly. "So was yours."

Serena's words were sweet, but it hurt him deeply that she had shunned him for so long.

An uncomfortable silence settled between them.

"Well, I guess I'll be going," she said.

As often happens when pride sets in, Toby and Serena had decided to hide their true feelings. Toby was tempted to let her go, but just as she turned to leave, he heard himself say:

"Wait a minute."

"Yes, Toby."

"Why have you been avoiding me?"

"My father does not want me to associate with you. He said you have seaweed where your brains should be. I'm sure he didn't mean it. I tried to reason with him, but you know my father."

"Seaweed where my brains should be?"

For some reason the phrase struck them as very funny and they began to laugh. The tensions melted and they laughed, and laughed, and laughed some more.

"SERENA!"

The angry voice had come from the direction of the pod.

"SERENA," growled the voice again.

"Great Blue! I've got to go. It's Father. Good-bye, Toby."

"But . . ."

"I'm sorry, Toby, but I really have to go."

Their eyes met for a brief moment. Then Serena turned and swam away.

10

The pod had entered warmer waters.

Early one morning Serena slipped away to tell Toby that the halfway point had been reached. How the elders knew this was a mystery to both of them. No matter where they looked they could see only sky and waves joined at the curved edge of the horizon. They decided finally that it must be the change in water color from a deep blue to a blue-green streaked with violet that was proof of their position in the seemingly endless sea.

Brief though it was, Toby was grateful for Serena's visit. Yet it reminded him of how much he missed the company of other whales—the talk, the touching, the little things that he had always taken for granted before.

Finding his real voice was proving to be a much

longer, lonelier, and more difficult task than Toby had ever expected. He had sung every trill and turn, dip and bend, rise and spill. He had coaxed and eased and cajoled his voice through thousands of musical combinations, loud as a hurricane, soft as a breeze. He had listened to his inner ears, tuned into the sound of everything at once, and accepted his dreams. Yet he seemed no closer now to finding his real voice, the voice that balanced heart and mind, than the day he had left Arctic Bay.

It was night, late night. Though he was bone-tired, Toby could not go to sleep. The moon had inched its way up and over and partway down the night sky before he finally began to drift away to the place of dreams. A most enticing sound traveled over the waves of his sleeping mind. A melody so sweet and pure and natural that it could have been sung only by a goddess, perhaps only by Great Blue herself. He followed the sound to a valley on the seabed where the vegetation was lush and luminous. And there, in a clearing, set off against a bank of pure white sand, Toby caught sight of the most beautiful whale-creature he had ever in his life laid eyes upon!

Could it be? As he looked more closely, he came to realize that in shape at least, the beautiful whale was the exact image of Serena. It was in substance that she was like no other Great Winged Angel Toby had ever seen. Truly she was radiant. Her skin, her very being, seemed to be lighted by some inner source.

He called to her: "Serena? Is that you?"

Their eyes met for a flicker of a moment. Then, without haste, she turned and swam away.

"Serena? It's me—Toby."

He lost sight of her as she glided over the crest of a jagged coral reef. When he reached the crest of the ridge, she was still nowhere to be seen. Then the sound of her lovely voice came floating across the waves again and he followed. He saw before him a great archway so brightly luminous that it might have been constructed of mother-of-pearl. And just beyond the arch she faced him, beckoning.

"Toby." The creature seemed to whisper in Toby's ear, though she was still some distance away. "Come, Toby, it's me."

"Serena?" Toby swam toward her. He dared not blink for fear that she would disappear again. The archway gleamed with rainbow brilliance above him. The alluring creature was waiting just beyond the arch. She was smiling.

"Don't swim away," he begged her.

"I won't swim away," she promised. "Come quickly," she urged him. "Your real voice is over here."

She did not swim away, but a moment later—when the gates of the archway crashed closed behind him and the lovely female Great Winged Angel turned into a dead thing with hollow, sunken, ghostly eyes, and he was caught up in some vast, swirling current that was pulling him down toward the center of a deep circular basin—he wished she *had* swum away. Better yet, he wished he would never have seen her in the first place!

Toby churned with all his might against the current, but no matter how hard he swam, the swirling mass of water pulled him closer, closer to the center of the basin. It was a losing battle—still, he had to fight! He struggled to the surface to catch a breath. At the center of the basin was a black hole from which, some pounding inner instinct told him there would be no escape. He swam like a brave mother salmon against the stream, growing weaker, living only for the next breath, and the next, never knowing which one could be his last.

Then suddenly, from out of nowhere, came a voice into his mind: "Relax, Toby, before it's too late. Surrender to the sound!"

It was Thes!

"Help!" Toby gasped, going down for the last time.

"For the love of Great Blue, Toby, surrender!"

Toby remembered the night he had flown with Thes. He felt the familiar warm tingle in the back of his brain. He heard the sound of everything at once rising from somewhere deep within him.

"The sound of the spirit, Toby! Remember, the song has wings!"

Toby relaxed and surrendered to the music, and just as he was about to be washed down the black hole at the center of the basin, the sound waves increased in frequency and he rose up from the churning, bubbling cauldron of bad dreams.

Suddenly he found himself in a quiet, peaceful place with Thes there to greet him.

"Am I glad to see you!" Toby exclaimed.

Thes's colors adjusted to subtler hues, matching his more relaxed mood. "It's a lucky thing I happened to tune into your dream channel when I did. He almost had you, Toby. A moment later might have been too late."

"Had me?" thought Toby. "Who?"

"I had a hunch Diomeda was behind the recent drainage of the dream reserves. Now I am all but certain."

"Diomeda?" Toby asked.

"Diomeda, the Dream Eater as he has come to be known, was a benevolent spirit until he began to long for the physical life again."

"Since he could not create a real material presence, he had to be content with the appearance of a physical body which he could create simply by consuming and then projecting energy from the Stream of Dreams."

Suddenly a picture of Diomeda, the Dream Eater, popped into Toby's inner view. He was wearing a navy blue uniform with brass buttons and gold braiding at the shoulders. Sideways on his head was a hat that resembled a three-masted schooner at full sail. He was surrounded by endless acres of lawns and gardens. Beautiful maidens attended to his each and every need.

"It might have been amusing," said Thes, "if it had not been such a terrible waste of dream energy. By the time we found out about it the Dream Eater's simple desire for a physical body had become a mad craving for mastery over the entire material plane. Lo and behold, there he was in a quiet corner of the cosmos, all dressed up in human dreams. It was a disgrace to spirits everywhere. Of course, we would have sent him packing anyway, but it was the Dream Eater's greed that turned out to be his downfall. His body, though it was composed only of the dreams he had eaten, had given him a weight which our world could not support. The last we saw of Diomeda he was drifting down to earth. We don't know what has become of him or how he has managed to avoid our psychic probes. He must have tapped into some incredible energy source. If he has found a way to syphon off dreams on a massive scale, he will undoubtedly do his best to steal every dream on the planet."

"How can we stop him?" Toby wanted to know.

"Before we can even think about stopping him, we have to locate him. I will double my efforts in that regard. In the meantime it is doubly important that you be on your guard, Toby. If Diomeda tried once to steal your dreams, he will most likely try again." "There is only one way to protect yourself from the likes of Diomeda: your real voice. If there is a chink in your armor, the slightest flaw in your character, the Dream Eater will zero in and devour your dreams."

"But I haven't found my real voice yet," he moaned. "I've been looking all over. I'm afraid I'll never find it. And even if I do find it, how will I know?"

"Don't worry, Toby. Keep searching. You'll know when you find it and so will I. A real voice echoes throughout all creation."

Thes cocked his head to one side, as if listening to some faraway sound.

"I've got to go, Toby. Dreams are pouring out of one of our reservoirs. It must be Diomeda. As for your real voice, Toby, that is something you must do on your own. Your real voice is as individual to you as the marks on your tail. No one can tell you where to find it, and once you have found it, no one can take it away."

"What if the Dream Eater tries again before I'm ready, Thes?"

"Beware, Toby, but do not be afraid. I will look in on you as often as I can. There is so much to do. I must go. Good luck, my friend, and remember always: Swim with the Spirit."

Toby blinked and Thes vanished into the thin mist of dawn.

11

Toby was back to his usual routine of cruising apart from the pod and singing, when a sudden urge to dive grabbed him and took hold. He drew a deep breath and started down. Shafts of dancing sunlight accompanied him on the first stage of his journey, but the light grew dimmer as he descended beneath a coral reef to a netherworld of shadows.

Toby swam deeper, darker, for the longest time. He was beginning to wonder if he would ever reach bottom when, finally, though his eyes had not yet fully adjusted to the gloom, the seabed became faintly visible.

A school of neon fish swam by, lighting the barren, rock-strewn seascape. There seemed to be nothing on the ocean floor to have compelled such a deep dive. He was about to return to the surface when he

heard an unusual sound and swam to see where it was coming from. As he drew closer, Toby realized that the sound was a voice, singing.

It seemed to be coming from a large rock.

> *I got the Babaroos*
> *Deep water rushin' over me;*
> *I got the Babaroos*
> *Deep water rushin' over me;*
> *No matter where I look,*
> *Deep water's all I see . . .*

Toby searched briefly and found the true source of the music, a hole beneath the rock.

"Hello!" Toby called. "Anybody home?"

The song stopped and two beady, curious eyes peered out from the hole.

"Not just anybody, but I'm here. You wouldn't happen to be Toby Whale would you?"

"Well . . . er . . . ah . . . yes, I would," replied a very startled Toby. "And who would you happen to be?"

"King Crab's the name," said the eyes, emerging with the body of a gnarly old crab attached to them. "Thes said you'd be dropping by."

"You know Thes, too?" asked Toby, astonished.

"Indeed I do. Met him just the other night. And

bein' a Babaroos singing crab from a long line of such crabs, I promised my support for the cause. Thes sends his regards to you. Told me to tell you that things are a lot worse than he thought. Somethin' about the dream reserves dryin' up. Anyways, he won't be seein' you for a while. I guess organizin' the big musical extravaganza is takin' up all his time. Say, how'd you find this place anyway?"

"I don't really know," replied Toby. "One minute I was swimming along, minding my own business, then the next minute I was diving deeper than I ever have before. I heard your music and here I am."

The two stared in silence for a long time, knowing it was more than a mere twist of fate that had brought them together.

Toby had a question on his mind.

"King Crab? . . ."

"Call me K.C. I like that better."

"K.C., that music you were singing . . . it was like nothing I've ever heard. I was wondering . . ."

King Crab changed positions. "Go ahead, my whale."

"Have you found your real voice?" Toby paused. "I've been looking all over, but I can't seem to find mine anywhere."

"The real voice, you say . . ." King Crab thought

for a long moment. "No, Toby can't say as I have. What I got is the Babaroos, just like my daddycrab and his daddycrab before him."

"What's it like, K.C.? To have the Babaroos, I mean?"

"Well, now, let's see." He smiled, contemplating his favorite subject. "It's somethin' that rises up in yourself like a big wave." He pointed a big front claw at his lower portion. "And it works its way up, buildin' as it goes. Then it comes out like ... well, like this:

> *I got the Babaroos*
> *Down here the water moves so slow;*
> *Yeah, I got the Babaroos*
> *Down here the water moves so slow;*
> *When you reach rock bottom,*
> *You're 'bout as low as you can go ...*

"That's great, K.C.! Can you teach me how to sing the Babaroos?"

"The Roos is a feelin', Toby. Takes a long time to teach a feelin'."

"That's too bad, K.C. I don't have much time. I'm an air-breather."

"What a shame, Toby. I could chew the fat all day long. Don't get many visitors in these parts, you know. Welcome visitors, that is. Most of 'em would just as soon eat you as look at you. That's just the way it is down here."

Toby and King Crab spoke of many things, as musicians from different swims of life often do when they first meet. Then it was time for Toby to leave. In fact, he had stayed longer than his air supply would normally have allowed.

"Well, K.C., it sure was good meeting you, but I guess I've got to go."

"Maybe we'll meet up again someday, Toby. Kinda doubt it, though."

"Why's that, K.C.?"

"Truth is, Toby, I don't have long for this world. The pressure's finally startin' to weigh me down. Don't you worry about ol' K.C. now, Toby. Thes tells me I'm gonna be the lead singer in that big Babaroos band in the sky." He paused and a wistful look entered his eyes. "Come to think of it, Toby, maybe we will meet up someday, over on the other side."

"Sure do hope so, K.C."

"Well, my whale, as the saying goes: "Swim with the Spirit!"

"Swim with the Spirit, K.C. And thanks!"

The ascent to the surface seemed even longer than

the swim down, and by the time he reached the coral reef Toby was on the verge of blacking out. A few fearful, breathless moments later he burst through top water to the much needed air above.

12

Toby spewed a cloud of vapor and drew in a few deep breaths before looking around for the pod. The long rays of the late evening sun created a blinding glare to the west. To the north, south, and east he could see nothing but an endless expanse of waves and sky. He called out in his loudest voice. No answer came.

"I will not be lost for long," he assured himself.

He felt small, or was it that the sea had suddenly grown? Never before had it looked so vast and intimidating.

"They can't have gotten far," he reasoned. "I'll be near them before sundown." Instinct guided him south. He swam at a feverish pace. Speed would be needed to beat the fall of night.

His hopes did not fade even with the setting of the sun.

"They must surely have noticed my absence and taken up a search by now."

The words rang hollow. Even if the others were searching, what chance did they have of finding each other in the dark, vast, forbidding sea?

He swam in fear, on the edge of despair. All night he swam, until the first light of dawn. Finally, dead tired, he sank into a light and restless dream-filled sleep.

He awoke in a cold sweat before dawn. A dream was on the edge of his mind, a nightmare that he could not quite remember. He called out in the blackness, hoping the night current had carried him within earshot of the others. He listened, but heard no response. The search was on again, through the morning and into the afternoon with still no sign of his pod.

Though he knew it to be a fact, Toby could still not believe he was lost. Whales of Toby's kind never got lost. If this was a part of Thes's plan, it was a plan of which he wanted no part.

Dazed, confused, he began to sing a sad mournful song. One by one, his bad feelings were released. Pain and loneliness intermingled, then departed. Soon, only the song remained.

Having entered a new universe of music, Toby was unaware of the arrival of six strangers.

"Great set of pipes you got there, pal."

Startled, Toby opened his eyes to find himself snout to snout with a killer whale. Quickly glancing to the right, he spotted two more orcas, and to the left, two more again, and yet another behind him.

"I tell you, pal, your voice and my brains, we could make beautiful music together." The orca had a lopsided grin that showed a mouthful of sharp, jagged teeth. "Am I right?"

Five replies came in rapid succession: "Right, Murdo!" "Star Material!" "Top of the heap!" "No doubt about it!" "Numero Uno!"

The one called Murdo was obviously the leader of the pack. "You're one lucky leviathan, pal. You just happened to be in the right place at the right time. We're personal managers for some of the heaviest entertainers in the sea: the New Waves, Sting Ray, Cetus Seal, Ebb and Flo. If it weren't for us, nobody would've heard of any of 'em. Got a name? Yeah, you . . . I'm talkin to you."

"Who? Ah . . . me?" blustered Toby. "No. I mean yes. Toby. Toby Whale. My pod was swimming south. I mean they're around here someplace. Actually, I was . . ."

"Just the name, Tobe," Murdo butted in, "not the whole life history. Toby Whale, eh? We'll have to do something about that. A class act deserves a class name. Know what I mean? Somethin' dignified yet simple. Somethin' catchy that'll stick. Any bright ideas?"

The other killer whales thought for a while before one of them ventured to say: "How about somethin' with a sleek exotic sound? Maybe like Finaldo Cetacean?"

"Nice try, Thrash. It's dignified, but not simple enough. Anybody else?" Murdo asked.

"How about Humphrey Humpback?" said another of the pack.

"You gotta be kiddin', Strokes," Murdo scorned. "Wait a minute. I got it! This one's a real inspiration. It came to me out of the blue. Know what I mean? Just like *that*. What's say we call him ... the Prince of Whales!"

"Fresh, boss!" "Class all the way!" "Real catchy!" "Take it to the sandy bank!" "If that don't grab 'em, nothing will!"

"Glad you like it," said Murdo. "What do *you* think, Prince?"

Sensing that a negative reply might be hazardous to his health, Toby decided to be as diplomatic as possible. "I haven't really thought much about changing my name, but if I did, that would certainly be a good one. I'm honored you want to manage me, but I guess I should tell you that I already have a manager."

"Is that a fact?" So what's this so-called manager's name?" Murdo inquired.

"Thes," said Toby cautiously.

"Thes who?" came Murdo's cold response.

"Thes ... ah ... Ophilous?" said Toby, offering the first word that came to mind.

"Thes ... ah ... Ophilous? You whales ever hear of a personal manager who goes by the name of Thes ... ah ... Ophilous?"

"Not me, Murdo." "Uh-uh." "Can't say's I have." "Negative." "Thes ... ah ... who?" They spoke in cautious tones as if sensing that Murdo's anger might explode at any moment.

"Believe me, Prince." Murdo forced a lopsided smile. "If this Thes Ophilous character was worth hearin' about, we'd have heard of him. I'm offerin' you the chance of a lifetime: the chance to sing for royalty in a command performance before none other than the Grand Supreme Emperor of Paradise Caverns. This is it Prince: the chance to make your dreams come true. You'd be a fool to pass it up for some nobody that nobody's ever heard of. Listen, I'll tell you what. If this Thes Ophilous shows up we'll take care of him real good. Won't we, guys?"

The five orcas snickered and elbowed each other with the backs of their flippers.

Murdo continued, "Who knows? We might even cut him in on a piece of the action. All depends how we slice it. Know what I mean?"

Toby knew only too well what the orca had meant. So did the others, judging by the way they were guffawing and carrying on. Toby tried to smile, failed, tried again. Something might have registered. He wasn't sure. It was always a good policy to laugh when a killer whale was telling jokes.

"Whatever happens ..." Murdo moved closer. "You won't have to worry. We look out for our own. Whadda you say? We got a deal?"

Toby considered the possibility of explaining Thes and the mission to reach the humans with music, but those sharp white teeth and cold black eyes made him change his mind. Murdo would not understand.

"Well, Princy, what's it gonna be?"

Toby quickly weighed his options. They didn't weigh much. Either he could say yes to the orca's offer or risk taking what characters of Murdo's sort termed "the big plunge." Toby had heard lurid, gruesome tales of killer packs no bigger than this one taking on the largest of all whales, the mighty Blue. He wouldn't stand a chance.

"Come on, Prince. We ain't got all day." Murdo's flipper twitched impatiently. The killers were pressing in. Toby had to give an answer. Not just any answer. He had to come up with one that would keep him alive until such time as he could escape.

"I guess we've got a deal," said Toby, sculpting his features into a vague rendition of a smile.

"The Prince of Whales it is!" Murdo slapped Toby lightly on the cheek. The others gathered round to welcome him into the pack. "By the time we're through with you, Prince, you'll be one of the biggest fish—pardon the expression—in the big pond. Ain't that the truth?"

"One of the biggest!" "Bigger than big!" "Gigantic!" "Colossal!" "An absolute monster!"

"Welcome to the biz, Your Highness. Okay. Let's get a move on." Murdo turned and started to swim, motioning for Toby to join him. The five others took positions beside and beneath them. "What we're gonna ask you to do may seem a little strange at first. The place we're takin' you, Paradise Caverns . . . well, things are different there."

"Different?" Toby asked.

"Yeah." Murdo paused. "What can I say? Like, in

order to succeed there, you kind of have to adapt to a whole 'nother cultural esthetic. You never saw nothin' like it in your life. But believe me, Prince, you won't regret it when you're sashayin' down the Great Blue Way. Am I right or am I right?"

The others echoed Murdo's sentiments.

13

The next days were spent swimming toward Paradise Caverns. Murdo called it the entertainment capital of the Pacific Basin. According to him, an extinct breed of sea dwellers, the legendary Deepwalkers, had built a city beneath the sea. Many of the structures and monuments remained, including one known simply as the Source, a light at the bottom of the sea so brightly magnificent that sealife came from deep and shallow to bask and wallow there. The Emperor of Paradise Caverns had restored the long-vacant ruins, creating accommodations and entertainment grottos for the visitors when they were not bathing in the light of the Source.

Toby learned of places with colorful names such as the Sand Bar, the Dive Inn, and the Watering Hole, where the finest entertainers in the sea plied their stock and trade. It was said by one of the killer whales that the audiences, and especially the Emperor of Paradise Caverns, demanded only the best when it came to entertainment. It was implied that Toby had better learn the songs and lines that they were teaching him—or else!

Every word and gesture of Toby's show was planned to the last detail, each song practiced a hundred times and then a hundred more. Murdo seemed pleased with his progress, but Toby was ready to scream. Being a singing slave to a pack of orca song sharks was not for him. Secretly he was only biding time, waiting for a chance to escape.

Late one afternoon a storm swept in, forcing the group to seek refuge in the calmer waters below. The gloomy tropical waters had a curious effect on the killer whales. They swam in silence, each seeming content to be alone with his private thoughts. They appeared to have lost interest in Toby completely.

Toby used the unusual quiet spell to ponder his plight. Lost in thought, he was surprised to see that he had fallen behind the others. He could have caught up easily had he wanted to. Instead, he slackened his pace, allowing the distance between them to become even greater. Anxiously he watched them swim away until only the faintest shadow remained of them.

Moments later the killer whales disappeared into the oozy darkened gloom.

Toby froze, motionless, heart pounding, thoughts of freedom streaking through his brain. The odds for escape were stacked heavy against him. Few whales could match orca speed and agility, and Toby had seen their uncanny knack of locating even the smallest objects with echo soundings. Still, another chance like this could be a long time coming again. It was now or never!

Toby turned and swam for all he was worth, staying submerged as long as he possibly could. Each ascent to the surface would cost precious time. When he could hold out no longer, he swam up for air. The storm raged in full fury. Thunder shook the water. Wind whipped the surface into a harried frenzy. Rain hissed down in a constant barrage. Lightning crackled, once, twice, three times, while Toby tried to catch a single breath. When he dove back down to the calmer waters, he could only pray that he had not altered course.

He churned on, the sweet hope of freedom spurring him to a second and then a third wind. He swam until he could swim no more. Exhausted, he looked back for the first time. The killers whales were nowhere to be seen. The storm had ended. The sun was now visible through breaking clouds. After a brief rest he continued at a slower pace, conserving the little energy that remained. He headed west until nightfall, plowing on through the night and well into the next day.

The pod had most likely reached the winter place by now, but where that might be was a mystery. By late that afternoon Toby was so drained of energy that his body was numb; his eyelids felt like anchors. He was seeing double, then triple, then nothing but a blur.

Finally he fainted into a long, deep sleep.

14

"Toby Whale. Message for Toby Whale."

The voice jarred Toby awake. Moments later a small black whale swam into view.

"Toby Whale. Message for ... Oh, is that you, Toby?"

"Yes, it's me," replied Toby, instantly regretting the admission. He had been too trusting. He should have found out more about the little whale's business before answering any questions, but he had still been half asleep.

"I have been looking all over for you," said the messenger. "Pilot Whale, Missing Sealife Brigade, M.S.B. Your loved ones contacted us and I was sent to find you. We are trained in such matters, and as our motto says: 'We always find our fish.'"

"My loved ones?" Toby was now fully awake and

excited at the prospect of being reunited with his pod.

"But of course," replied the messenger. "I've come to take you to them. If we hurry, we can be there by midday."

"What are we waiting for!" Toby exclaimed.

Toby liked pilot right away. The two shared music as a common interest. Pilot seemed not the least surprised to learn of Toby's capture by the killer whales. Murdo and his whales were known throughout the area and many fine young singers had fallen into their clutches. In fact, Pilot himself had been imprisoned at Paradise Caverns for nearly twenty-four cycles of the moon before finally managing to escape.

After forcing Pilot into a year of labor as an entertainer, the orcas had made it appear as if he owed them for everything, from the chambers where they had held him prisoner, right down to the water he had displaced. Hopelessly in debt, Pilot had no choice but to continue singing, paying back what he never owed, and never catching up. It was a vicious cycle and a bitter experience that had robbed Pilot of any desire to sing for a long time.

"Singers are no more than slaves to them," Pilot confided. "They don't have to hurt you. They make you a prisoner of your own fear."

The noonday sun was directly above them when Pilot pointed a flipper in the direction of a small, ring-shaped coral island and announced, "We're nearly there. Your loved ones are just beyond that ridge."

Toby's heart pounded, the excitement almost too much to bear.

"Down here," said Pilot, leading the way through a narrow passage in the jagged coral reef.

"Welcome to Paradise, Princy!"

Toby looked up to see the most shocking sight of his young life: Murdo and the killer whales!

"Nice work, Pilot," said Murdo. "Knew you'd come through."

Pilot responded in a low, almost guilty tone: "Sure, Murdo. Don't go too hard on him. He's had a rough few days."

"Not half as tough as the next few days are gonna be," joked Thrash. The other whales began to snicker, but when they saw that Thrash's attempt at humor was not appreciated by Murdo, they clammed up fast.

"Don't worry about Princy," said Murdo to Pilot. "You don't think we'd do any damage to our star entertainer here, do you?"

Pilot swam by Toby and whispered, "I still owe 'em." Then he turned and swam away.

Murdo shook his head from side to side.

"You made a bad mistake, Prince. You underestimated us. We had a deal. Nobody backs out of a deal with us. Ain't that right, fellas?"

Murdo's whales replied in suitably indignant tones: "Right." "Can't back out on us." "A deal's a deal." "Shouldn't oughta have done that." "No way."

"Like I was sayin'," Murdo went on, "we put all that energy into gettin' your act together and you turn around and slink off like some slimey mud-crawler. It was a real slap in the kisser. Then we got to thinkin'. Maybe Princy just got lost. Maybe it was somethin' we said. Maybe a lot of things. Anyway, we decided to let bygones be bygones. Everybody's entitled to one mistake. Right?"

The others were right on cue: "Yeah, so he made a mistake." "Maybe Princy just got lost." "Maybe he got magnesia or something." "We don't want to hurt nobody." "Let's give the Prince a break."

"There, ya see Prince," said Murdo. "Whaddya say? No hard feelin's, right? We'll make a fresh start. But we can't have our singers galavantin' all over creation. Nex' time we brain ya, understand? I mean fair's fair, right?"

Disheartened, with no hope for escape, the best Toby could manage was a feeble, "Whatever you say, Murdo."

For a split second Murdo looked genuinely concerned.

"Hey, take it easy, Prince. You look like somethin' the catfish dragged in. Cheer up! Everything's gonna work out great. Just like I said. You'll feel better once you get settled in. Come on; we'll show you round the Caverns."

15

Paradise Caverns was teeming with sealife of every description. Never before had Toby seen such a startling array of strange creatures in one place at one time. Exotic, luminous devilfish swam by, proudly displaying their brightly colored skins. Blue whales the size of tankers chatted amiably in deep, resonant voices. Shoals of silver darters darted, clownfish clowned, and sailfish sailed by with nothing more on their minds, it would seem, than the pursuit of pleasure.

At first glance Paradise Caverns seemed to live up to its name, but as they swam through the complex maze of underwater caves and half-submerged caverns, Toby began to notice that all was not well with the sealife there. Some swam slowly, aimlessly, as if each flick of their tails caused them pain. Others looked worn and spent, dead to the world, their glazed, sunken eyes crying out for compassion. They lurked in darkened corners: the blinded, the crippled, the misshapen waifs whose color had faded to a pale gray. Any dreams that these poor creatures might once have had had long since vanished. A chill crept over Toby and he shuddered.

"Don't worry about *them*," said Murdo. "They don't know from nothin'. Been floatin' around like that for years. Don't know where they came from, but they're sure not goin' nowhere. Don't eat. Don't sleep. Don't talk. All they do is float around lookin' ugly. Wouldn't hurt a guppy, though."

After a short time they came to the edge of a deep circular basin which Toby estimated to be about a third the width of Arctic Bay. A strange light oozed from the center of the basin which was dotted with the shadows of those who had gathered to bathe in the light of the Source.

"That little baby keeps us in business," said Murdo proudly. "The light comes from somewhere deep beneath the basin. The true believers say that baskin' in that light makes you live forever. You'd have to be incredibly dimwitted to swallow that, but there's somethin' very, very awesome down there. That you can believe."

Toby's eyes were focused on the eerie changing

light at the center of the basin. He could see the silhouettes of countless sea beings. From the basin emerged a shadowy figure, a dolphin. It looked like Chetly, the dolphin Toby had sung with, but in some strange way it did not look like him.

"Chetly, is that you?" Toby asked.

The dolphin did not answer.

"Chetly, it's me—Toby—remember? We sang together?"

The dolphin looked at Toby with dull, almost sightless eyes.

"Toby?" A small, weak smile visited his face, then vanished. "Yeah, now I remember."

"Are you all right?" Toby asked.

"Huh? Yeah ... sure, like fine. I found the source. The Source ..."

Chetly's face went blank again and he turned and drifted away.

"You know that mug?" Murdo asked.

"I knew him ..." Toby answered, watching Chetly disappear into the crowd.

"We'd call that 'Enlightened.' " Murdo grinned lopsidedly.

The other whales added: "All lit up." "Tight with the light." "Got a serious glow on." "Sourced out!" He has *seen* the light!"

"They say that basking in the Source is a way to peace and tranquility in a troubled world. If that's peace and tranquility, who needs it? Come on. This place gives me the creeps."

Murdo led them through a gigantic underwater archway to a place from which the basin and many rows of sandstone structures could be seen. They surrounded the basin row on row in a way that reminded Toby of the city of humans he had visited with Thes. In fact, Paradise Caverns looked remarkably like a human city. The thought pounded on Toby's inner ears: "An entire human city must have sunk into the sea!"

The closer Toby looked, the more certain he became. Paradise Caverns had been built around the basin and the Source. Yet the light from the Source was unlike any in the city he had visited with Thes. Something else puzzled him. The human Deepwalkers were long gone, but the caverns had a strange newness about them, a ghostly vitality. There was more to Paradise Caverns than met the eye, much more.

Soon they arrived at a large sandstone complex which Murdo said was reserved for entertainers in residence. The only entrance was guarded by a surly great white shark.

"Gnarl baby," said Murdo to the shark. "Meet the Prince of Whales. Now don't go spillin' any of his royal blood unless he gets out of line. Know what I mean?"

Gnarl grinned knowingly, showing four rows of broken teeth. "I catch your drift." The shark attempted to wink, but both of his eyes closed at the same time.

"Entertainers in residence," thought Toby. "That's a laugh. This is a prison and I'm a prisoner of fear. Pilot told the truth about *that* at least."

Toby's lodgings were quite luxurious, consisting of three large adjoining chambers, one above water and the other two below. The water in the lowest chamber was stocked with shrimp. Small portholes provided a good view of one of the main streams of Paradise Caverns, the Great Blue Way.

"Terrific place you got here," Murdo enthused. "Wall to wall kelp. Starfish on the door. Hope you appreciate it. Strokes, you and Crusher stay here and run through the show with Prince. I'll go down to the Grotto and make arrangements for tonight. No sense wastin' any more time. The rest of you come with me."

During Murdo's absence Toby rehearsed his act. He remembered all his lines and every song and every stupid joke that Murdo and the killer whales had taught him, but he could not keep his mind on singing. His thoughts kept drifting to the strange circumstances that had befallen him.

Murdo returned a short while later and announced: "We're on tonight, the Emperor's gonna be there. Everybody's gonna be there. Hope you got your act together, Prince. This is gonna be the biggest night of your life. Now let's take it from the top!"

Murdo took his job very seriously. He was not satisfied until every last detail of the Prince of Whales show was perfect. After rehearsing the act at least a dozen more times, they swam down the Great Blue Way, arriving at a large cave that led into the Famous Grotto. Murdo was first to enter, followed by Toby and the ever-present pack of yes-whales. Fin, a small, sly, slippery looking fellow in a genuine sharkskin suit, swam over to exchange greetings.

"So this is the young singer you've been telling me about," said the shark in a rasping whisper that came from the corner of his mouth. Then, speaking to Toby alone, he said, "Ya know, Prince, this is the big time, the deep leagues; we play for keeps down here. Hope you're not in over your head."

Though said in a joking manner, Fin's remarks did nothing for Toby's confidence. He was already having a hard bout with stage fright. And he knew only too well that if he did not perform up to expectations, he would most certainly suffer some dire consequence.

It was time to face the music.

16

The light in the Famous Grotto took on a peculiar dreamlike quality and a voice from above announced:

"Welcome one and all. Tonight the Famous Grotto is proud to present ... direct from a triumphant engagement at the Sand Bar ... The Seal You Can Feel ... The one ... the only ... Cetus Seal!" The capacity audience erupted as Cetus Seal bounded on stage and began to sing his upbeat opening number, "Sink or Swim."

> *When life is looking grim*
> *Day in day out day in day out day in*
> *Can't get by on a whim*
> *Day in day out day in day out day in*
> *The surface you can't skim*
> *Day in day out day in day out day in*
> *It's either sink or swim ...*

The seal belted out the fast montuna with the calm self-assurance of a seasoned entertainer. His voice was not the best that Toby had ever heard, but his delivery was smooth, his timing impeccable, his phrasing faultless. An instrumental solo allowed him an opportunity to display his remarkable acrobatic dancing skills. By the time he reached the musical bridge section the audience was crowding the amphitheater stage a hundred deep on all sides.

> *Yes, we struggle to survive,*
> *But that's life; we have to live it*
> *And it's hard to stay alive*
> *Without love and so we give it.*
> *That's the chance we have to take*
> *In the game that we must play*
> *When we live for each day*
> *And let our hearts show the way . . .*

When the song ended in a flurry of fanfare, the audience exploded. Cetus Seal's electrifying performance only added to Toby's stage fright. He felt dreadful, flukes and flippers shaking out of control, cold sweat dripping from every pore.

"Thank you! Thank you!" yelled Cetus Seal above the din. "Thank you very much! What an audience! You're great! I love ya! What a band! Let's hear it for the High Seas Orcastra! Take a bow! Take a bow! Thank you! Thank you! Thank you very much!"

Some of the band members rose from the orchestra pit to take their bows. There were drumfish, trumpetfish, electric guitarfish, and a bedraggled assortment of odd-looking musical creatures that Toby could not identify.

The Cetus Seal show continued. Toby heard, but he did not hear. He saw, but he did not see. So many thoughts were swimming through his mind that it was like having no thoughts at all. By the time his attention returned, Cetus Seal was about to introduce his last song.

"We've got a great lineup of entertainment planned for you this evening. I'll be coming back to do another set." The seal smoothed back the fur on his head with a flipper. The audience hooted with delight. "I ask you," he purred, "what could be better than that? No, but seriously, seafolks, coming up next is a guest who puts on a whale of a show. He's been packin' 'em in like sardines everywhere he plays. No offense to all you sardines out there. I am speaking of none other than the Prince of Whales!"

The audience responded with a smattering of applause.

"And of course our own supreme, sublime, royal majestic highness, the Emperor of Paradise Caverns, will be making his entrance any moment now, so don't you go away. You're such a great audience. They pay good clams at the Grotto, but to tell you the truth, I'd play here just for the halibut. Give yourself a nice round of applause. That's it. Cod bless ya. You're great. I love ya. I'd like to leave you with a song by my good friend Jules Manatee. The beautiful ballad, 'You Only Want Me ...'" He paused for dramatic effect. "'... When You Need Me.'"

After a short musical introduction, Cetus Seal began to sing.

> My mind is in a jumble,
> I lose my voice and mumble;
> I've got it bad and that's no lie.
> My thoughts are tight and tangled,
> My edgy nerves are jangled,
> And you're the reason that I cry ...
>
> You only want me when you need me;
> I want you every night and day.
> You only need me when you want me;
> I want a love that's gonna stay ...

There was no question that Cetus Seal could sell a song. When it ended, the crowd thundered its approval as Cetus bounded to the edge of the stage and dove off. They called for an encore, but the seal did not oblige.

Murdo shouted, "It's a tough act to follow, Prince, but you can do it. Just keep your cool and do the show just like we planned it. You're gonna knock 'em dead!"

Just then the lights dimmed; the drumfish rolled; the audience hushed as high above them the Emperor of Paradise Caverns emerged. Proud, erect, in human form, the Emperor strode to the edge of the royal balcony. He raised his hand and smiled down on his subjects, bathing them in a nimbus of reflected glory. He gleamed with a radiance beyond that of any mortal. His dress was more opulent than that of any king. His jewel-encrusted cape and crown were of such hue and sparkle as to dazzle the eye. The audience gasped in awe.

"Great Blue!" The truth came crashing into Toby's mind like a rogue wave. "Either that's the Dream Eater or I'm a humpbacked krill!" He flashed back to the vast, swirling current that had almost been the death of him. He remembered the beautiful Great Winged Angel, the exact image of Serena, and how it had changed into a ghastly, decaying dead thing before his eyes. "Thes said that only my real voice could protect me," Toby thought. "I guess it's just my tough luck that I haven't found it. Thes!" He cried out with all the power that his mind possessed. "Thes! Where are you when I need you?" Thes did not answer. He would not answer. Something told Toby that whatever was going to happen, he would have to face it on his own. Fear gripped him as it never had before.

The excitement caused by the Emperor's entrance had begun to fade when the voice from above announced:

"Let's have a royal welcome for the Prince of Whales!"

17

Anot so gentle nudge from Murdo made Toby painfully aware that it was his turn to perform.

"This is it," he said. "Get out there and do your thing!"

"Do it, Princy!" "Make some waves!" "Get down with your deep self!" "Break a fluke!" "Show the world!"

Somewhere in the back of his brain, Toby heard the introduction to his first song. Numb with fright, he swam out to face the audience and began to sing:

> *In my dream we were together,*
> *Words so sweet we did proclaim,*
> *Thoughts of love I did envision,*
> *My desires were aflame . . .*

The first time Toby dared to look out at the audience he was stunned to see that they seemed to be enjoying his performance. Toby's voice was cracking and wavering on the long notes, but it didn't seem to matter. Even the Dream Eater seemed amused.

In my imagination
We performed a perfect play,
Just a simple act of loving
And we were swept away,
Swept a-way . . .

After what seemed like hours the song ended to spirited applause. The loud flipper flapping, clicks, and whistles amazed Toby, but annoyed him all the same. The audiences in his dreams would never put up with such bad singing.

"Is this what I practiced for?" he asked himself.

Toby's next song was a wishy-washy midstream ballad, "Moist and Mellow Over You." Murdo called it a real gusher, but it was without doubt the worst song Toby had ever heard. As it ended, a strange sensation came over Toby. He drew in his breath to begin his next song when a sudden stream of scattered images flooded his senses.

Brujon appeared, as clearly as if he were there.

"Toby," he said in a stern tone, "only the quick of wit and stout of heart survive."

Toby blinked and the image of his father was replaced by that of Maestro Baleeni. "Some call it talent, but I choose to call it courage. The courage to be yourself."

"No," Toby sighed. "No . . . go away."

Toby cleared his throat and was about to sing when he saw an Iron Beast and heard Thes say: "If there is a chink in your armor, a flaw in your character, the Dream Eater will devour your dreams."

Other memories came and vanished, visions of Luma, Aunt Undeen, Chetly, King Crab, and Serena.

As if awakened from a dream, Toby looked out at the audience and up to the self-proclaimed Emperor of Paradise Caverns.

"This whole place is nothing but a mad fantasy," he thought. "Paradise Caverns, the Famous Grotto, the Emperor. Nothing but a sham. A sick, disgusting dream. And what of me? Am I to be a slave? A coward, afraid to stand by my convictions? If I can't be a free whale, I'm nothing. Nothing! I must sing my own music. Only I can make my dreams come true."

Just then a great, godlike, reverberating voice pierced Toby's inner ears.

"Hear me well, Dream Singer! Those were fine thoughts. Courageous thoughts indeed. But I will tell you now that you are not free. Nor will you ever be. From now on your dreams belong to the Emperor of Paradise Caverns!"

"You have no power over me, Dream Eater," thought Toby.

"So, you know my true identity. Then you are an even bigger fool than I thought. You have seen the colorless shells of my victims and still you dare to defy me? Then, truly, you must be the biggest fool I have ever seen!"

"It is you who is the fool, Dream Eater. I suggest you just float away to wherever it is that blowfish float to."

Diomeda laughed. "Your ignorance amuses me. It will be a pleasure to devour the dreams of a spirit's apprentice, but I am not hungry just now. Get on with your show as planned and spare us your little heartfelt song. We are not interested."

"I will sing whatever music I please."

"We shall see about that!" boomed the Dream Eater.

He sucked in his breath, growing to twice the size he was before, and let out a storm of terror, a tidal wave of dread that raged through Toby's brain like a thousand nightmares. It left him cold, shaking, gasping for air.

"Now get on with your show, Prince of Whales. The audience is becoming restless and so am I."

"WE WANT MUSIC! WE WANT MUSIC! WE WANT MUSIC!" the audience chanted, filling the Famous Grotto with their anger.

Murdo, Fin, Gnarl, and the killer whales were swimming toward him.

Just as they reached him, Toby began to sing. They stopped in their wakes as if a wall of music blocked their path. The audience was stunned into silence. It was Toby's song they heard, but it was their song, too—every song they had ever heard, every emotion they had ever felt. Helplessly they listened as Toby sang—each note reaching deeper into the forgotten hollows of their inner selves:

Water pure air so clean
Is a vision I have seen
And I know I'm not alone
We can find a way . . .

"You push me too far, Dream Singer! Do you really think your wretched little song can protect you against my mighty arsenal?"

The Dream Eater expanded to three times his former size and released a sound and fury of such devastating force that Toby reeled from the impact. Evil creatures—half shark, half man—beckoned him to enter the jaws of death. Bloodsucking remoras converged upon him, attaching themselves to his skin, his face, his mouth, his eyes. Electric eels swarmed around him. Fear gripped him, but Toby sang on:

> *Iron Beasts come to kill*
> *Take our lives but not our will*
> *And I know I'm not alone*
> *We can find a way . . .*

"Surrender!" screamed the Dream Eater. "Surrender or lose your precious dreams!"

"I'll never surrender to you, Dream Eater," answered Toby. "You are nothing but a bad dream."

"A bad dream am I?"

Diomeda grew to five times his former size and hurled a barrage of images more terrifying than Toby had ever imagined, even in his wildest dreams. Giant squid wrapped tentacles around him and squeezed. Monstrous seahawks swooped down, blood dripping from their huge gaping beaks, claws slashing. Nine-headed serpents boiled the water with their acrid breath. Snakes writhed and slithered over him, tongues darting, fangs spewing poisonous venom.

"It's only a dream," Toby told himself. "A bad dream." He could feel his color fading, the strength of his convictions faltering. Still, he gathered strength and sang on:

> *Humankind learn to share*
> *Music is our only prayer*
> *And I know I'm not alone*
> *We can find a way . . .*

"Soon, Dream Singer, the humans *will* learn to share! Their bodies, their minds, their dreams . . . selfish as they are, they will share everything with me! Soon they too will know Diomeda's wrath!"

With that, the Dream Eater extended himself to the very limit of his resources. Molten lava oozed up from the seabed, clogging Toby's pores, choking off his breath. Acid rain fell, raising hissing billows of foul black steam. Cities crumbled. Forests burned. Glaciers melted. Oceans boiled, then dried like blood on a wound. A blinding glare of white-hot light blazed across the endless cosmos and mushroom clouds rose to the heavens. And there, in the murky clouds of darkness, all that remained was a whale lying helpless on the scorched surface of what was once the ocean floor. It was the last whale, a dying whale.

"Great Blue, help me . . . help me. No . . . it can't be. No. Please. The whale is me. The whale is *me!*"

Toby watched in horror as his flesh peeled from

his bones. There was an agonized scream, a scream that came not from the beached whale but from himself. He could see his vital organs began to dissolve. He shut his eyes to block the vision, but it did no good. Death was coming—blackness, nothingness, the death of Toby's dreams. All that remained of the beached whale, the last whale, was a skeleton—dry, dead, white bones.

18

From out of the silent emptiness came a voice, a distant whisper.

"You are mine, Dream Singer."

With barely the strength to focus his eyes, Toby looked upward into the darkness. Diomeda was there, glowering down, triumphant. Yet the Dream Eater's aura had dimmed. His jeweled cape and crown had lost much of their former splendor. The battle had taken a heavy toll.

"Could it be," Toby wondered, "that I still have half a chance?"

He thought of those who loved him, those who had helped him, those who had lost their lives and their dreams.

"If I am dead, Dream Eater, then I have nothing to lose. If I am alive, then I would rather be dead then be a slave to the likes of you."

Even as he spoke, Toby could feel a change taking place, a transformation. His voice was not the voice of a whale who had died. It was the voice of a whale who had never really lived before. A voice that balanced heart and mind. A voice no evil could withstand. At last, Toby had found his real voice!

> Troubled seas, troubled land
> One last chance to take a stand
> And I know I'm not alone
> We can find a way . . .

Slowly the Dream Eater began to fade, shrinking, melting, his body aging, receding, vanishing before his own eyes. He shrieked, dismayed, hurling a spray of pale visions that dissipated like tears in the sea.

"My body!" he croaked. "You've stolen my body!"

"It was not yours to begin with, Dream Eater. The dreams you used to make it belonged to others."

"They are mine! Mine by divine right! Mine because I make them mine!" The last of Diomeda's strength was leaving him. "I'll get you, Prince of Whales. I promise you: I will have my revenge!"

Diomeda's body, now a thin, frail, ghostly shape, drifted upward and disappeared.

The audience yawned, stretched, and smiled at each other as if they were awakening from a long sleep. Color streamed back into their bodies and into the surroundings—true color, natural color. Toby swam among them, singing the ancient song of protection he had learned from Maestro Baleeni. Until now, the true purpose of that soothing song had been forgotten.

They watched and listened, and one by one they began to sing. And as Toby swam out the main passage to what had once been the Great Blue Way, they began to follow; Murdo, Fin, Gnarl, Cetus, the High Seas Orcastra, and all the sealife followed and joined their voices with the song. By the time they had reached the outwaters, the mighty chorus was a thousand voices strong.

When they reached open ocean a light, like a flame with no center, appeared before Toby's eyes.

"You have done well, my friend."

Toby could not pinpoint the source of the voice. It seemed to come from everywhere at once.

"Thes?"

"Yes, Toby, it's me. I won't bother to make myself visible."

"Thes, where have you been? I thought you were never coming back."

"I'm sorry about what happened. I couldn't find you. Diomeda's entire domain was hidden beneath a force field of illusion. Had your real voice not penetrated the shield, I might never have found you."

"The light in the basin ... What is it?" asked Toby, by mind alone.

"The last vestige of another human society that lost its way. This is not the first time man has pushed our planet to the brink of disaster. It happens just like clockwork every million years or so. Somebody figures out how to transform the atoms of a light element into those of a heavier element. It's a reaction that gives off tremendous energy, but one error in judgment and the world goes up in flames. Then the cycle begins anew, discovering languages, religions, nations. But they're not going to blow themselves and us up again. Not this time. Not if we have anything to say about it."

"But the Dream Eater said he would return. He is out to make the humans his slaves."

"That is all the more reason, Toby, why we have to reach the humans before the Dream Eater gets to them. The humans are a stubborn lot, and once their hearts and minds are in the right balance, Diomeda will be powerless against them. Now the real work begins. Many have joined our ranks, both on land and sea, but so many more have yet to be awakened. I will be searching through the night for last-minute recruits. We advance at dawn. It is my hope that others will share our vision and lend their voices as we go along. Your job, Toby, is to lead this chorus. Seek out humans and sing. If our plan succeeds, we will start a revolution of music that will live forever. The survival of every creature on this planet rests in the balance. Good luck, Toby, and may you always swim with the Spirit!"

Before Toby had a chance to think another thought, Thes had disappeared. Finding his real voice was one thing. Leading a chorus of sealife against the hardhearted humans was another. He had no time to reflect. The chorus was getting restless. It was as if they knew that they, too, had become part of a greater plan.

A battle of music was about to be waged.

PART THREE

PART
THREE

19

The first human being to hear the chorus was an old man, a passenger aboard a large luxury liner, who, having been awakened by a dream, had risen early with the intention of photographing the first light of dawn. This, he realized, could be his last voyage and he wanted to make the most of it. There he stood in near darkness, camera ready, on the sun deck at the bow of the ship, as the first rays of sunlight peaked over a hazy horizon.

The sound came softly at first, rising through the mist and with the sun, a beautiful and compelling sound that caused him to strain his eyes in an effort to find the source. Through a brief opening in the mist he caught a glimpse of indistinct shapes in the water below, quickly covered again by a waft of dewy haze. The rising sound was the only evidence that what he had seen had not been a mirage.

Aroused by the music, other passengers dressed quickly and came to the ship's railings. Within minutes the mist had lifted and they could clearly see the chorus surrounding them. No one said a word. Their eyes, ears, and mouths gaped open and the song touched their hearts.

By the next day the whole world was buzzing. Reports of singing marine life streamed into the newspapers and television stations, and people flocked to the seas and shores to see for themselves if the stories were true. Scientists came to seek a reasonable explanation. Recording engineers came with tape recorders. Music lovers and children came in small boats to listen and join voices with the chorus.

Thes had worked his magic on land as well as at sea, and those humans who lived inland could not ignore Nature's symphony. They heard elephants trumpeting, wolves howling, geese honking, birds singing, bullfrogs croaking, monkeys chattering, hyenas laughing, and all the wildlife of the world singing together in perfect harmony.

Those who listened with their hearts needed no explanation. They knew what the song was about. The children knew, and the poets and the clowns. But those who listened only with their minds still hid behind their disbelief. They made up theories. They built soundproof rooms and gave their pets away.

They put earplugs in their ears and shot guns at birds, cut down trees, uprooted flowers, and buried their lawns in cement. They played their car radios loud and sprayed for insects, but they could not escape the sound of Nature's mighty chorus.

In an effort to find a reasonable explanation for the sounds, the world's greatest thinkers convened at the World Council headquarters. Business executives discussed the profit potential. Military advisors planned the possibility of armed intervention. Then they stood before the assembly to present their theories. The chairman of the board could not explain, nor could the admiral, the marine biologist, or the noise pollution expert. Presidents, diplomats, doctors, lawyers, kings and queens all tried, but none could provide an answer.

When they had exhausted all their theories, the Secretary General of the World Council addressed the spectators of the proceedings who had watched from the balconies and listened to the long-winded debate.

"We have tried and failed to explain the cause of the worldwide epidemic of sounds. We now invite those of you who have listened to the discussions to offer your explanations."

At first none of the spectators dared to say a word. After all, what could they possibly add to the thoughts of the world's greatest thinkers? Then a small girl raised her hand and rose to address the council.

"Yes, little girl," said the Secretary General.

All eyes turned with great bemusement.

"I can explain," she said. "It's so simple. The song is about sharing. We have taken too much and not given enough in return. Listen with your hearts and you will understand."

Then the little girl sat down.

"Thank you for your wise comments, little girl," said the Secretary General. "We will discuss them at our next meeting."

Everyone but the little girl burst into gales of laughter.

"Listen with our hearts! But isn't that what our ears are for?" remarked one of the spectators, thinking he was very clever.

And the laughter went on and on, echoing around the great hall.

When they saw, through their merriment, that the little girl was not sharing in their folly, a few of the people who were sitting nearby turned to congratulate her for the comic relief she had provided.

"Thank you for making us laugh, little girl."

"You have taken the edge off a very serious situation."

"You are very cute. Isn't she adorable!"

Then they laughed some more.

When the conference ended, they still were laughing, temporarily blocking the sounds of Nature's song. They could not admit that a child might know more than the greatest thinkers in the world. But when they returned to their soundproof rooms and remembered the little girl's words, they began to ponder. What if she was right? Maybe, just maybe, the answer *was* that simple. Some opened their hearts, just a crack, to test the little girl's theory, and soon they too began to understand.

The others, the ones who refused to listen, put up a good fight. They closed their minds and locked in their feelings. They counted their money and waited for the song to go away. They held their ground and hid behind their old beliefs because they were afraid. Afraid to admit they had been wrong. Afraid they would have to listen.

20

Sealife came from the depths to join the chorus. They came to sing to human hearts. They came to help free the seas of tyranny. Each day the song grew stronger and more and more humans were awakened to the cause.

Hearing that a chorus of singing sealife was out to change the world, a distant whale pod swam for many miles to join with them. The pod was Toby's own! The outburst of joy that happened that day could not be contained. At last Luma and Brujon had found their son. They laughed at the sleepless nights and cried over the endless days of searching. Only Maestro Baleeni had no time for a flood of emotions. He could not wait to add his voice to the musical throng.

Serena waited patiently for the crowd around Toby to clear. Then she approached him.

"I missed you, Toby."

Her simple words penetrated Toby's deepest regions. Memories of their childhood together rushed his senses and love touched him as it never had before. Love for Serena, for his parents, for Maestro Baleeni, Murdo, and the elders. Love for Thes, the chorus, and all the wild things. Love for Nature and even for the humans.

Toby and Serena gazed into each other's eyes, love overflowing. They might have gazed for days had it not been for the sudden commotion. Something was wrong. Terribly wrong. The chorus had stopped singing. Bedlam had broken loose.

21

Toby scanned the horizon.

Great Iron Beasts were coming—floating factories, like so much litter on the sea, still distant, but closing fast. The faint but unmistakable odor of whale flesh spurred memories of the night he had flown with Thes and had seen one of the death ships for the first time. The true test was near.

Toby began to swim among the chorus.

"Hold strong," he urged. "Sing as one."

Instinct told him that only he could hold them together. If he lost his courage, his dream and the dream of many others would be consumed by the Iron Beasts.

"Surrender to the song, not the humans."

He was afraid, but could not let it show. He sang from the depths of his soul, pausing to give comfort to those whose fear was greater than his own.

"Sing from the heart," he told them. "From the heart."

Maestro Baleeni was the first to respond. He sang as if a volcano of controlled emotions had erupted. His voice combined with Toby's, casting courage to those around them, giving strength to even the faintest heart.

The chorus members who had turned to flee stopped in their wakes. No longer fearful, they rejoined the others. They sang for Nature. They sang for their very lives.

The death ships were not the only vessels converging in a steadily shrinking circle around the chorus. Rowboats, cabin cruisers, yachts, and trawlers were coming from shoreward, carrying people with good intent and bad. Still, the chorus held their position and bravely sang on.

Most of the people in the small craft meant no harm. They had seen the factory ships and knew their murderous purpose. They leaned from their boats and shouted to the men in the ships: "Stop! Can't you hear the music? Are you deaf? Stop! In the name of God, stop!" Some brave souls steered their small boats into the path of the oncoming ships, but the death ships kept coming.

The men on the Iron Beasts watched as the small boats tried to block their course, but they did not stop. They could hear the brave souls shouting, but they did not listen. They had come to do a job and they meant to do it. This was a whaler's dream come true, and they were not about to see it ruined by a few foolish people. They watched as their ships rammed the small boats, sending the poor souls flying into the sea. Still they did not stop. What did it matter if a few whale lovers lost their lives? It would be no fault but their own.

Seafolk and humans alike went to the rescue. The whalemen looked on as men, women, and children floundered helplessly in the cold sea, but they did not care. They could hear the chorus singing, but they did not listen. The sound was not music to their ears, but only another noise, like the rumbling engines of their deadly ships.

The captain of the fleet shouted orders to all the ships through giant loudspeakers: "MAN YOUR POSITIONS! AHEAD FULL! STAND BY TO ATTACK!"

The great, godlike, reverberating voice shot shivers up Toby's spine. It was the voice of Diomeda, the Dream Eater!

22

Nightmare, the flagship of the death fleet, now loomed so near that an ominous shadow covered the chorus and the pungent stench of decaying whale meat hung heavy in the still salt sea air. High above them whalemen scrambled to their battle stations. Toby could see the silhouette of the captain on the bridge, rigid, imposing.

"Yes it's me, Dream Singer. The captain, careless fellow, has somehow misplaced his dreams. A much worse fate is in store for you."

"HARPOONER! KILL THE ONE WHO LEADS THEM! FIRE WHEN READY!"

Toby watched the massive whaling gun swing slowly around and come to rest leveled straight at him. Serena was with him. Brujon, Luma, Maestro Baleeni, Murdo, and the killer whales swam to be by his side. He glanced at his loved ones hoping it was not for the last time. He could not let them down. He locked eyes with the young harpooner and he sang as he never had before. His voice and the voices of the chorus combined, growing louder, stronger. The harpooner, finger poised on the trigger, hesitated.

"WHAT ARE YOU WAITING FOR! I SAID FIRE AND I MEAN FIRE!" screamed Diomeda.

Toby saw nothing but the harpooner's eyes. He did not notice chorus members and people in small boats coming to form a circle around him. His eyes were fixed on the eyes of the harpooner, and if need be, he would sing until his dying breath.

"FOR THE LAST TIME!" bellowed the Dream Eater. "SHOOT TO KILL!"

Torn between his captain's wrath and his own sudden compassion, the harpooner could no longer hold the gaze of the young whale whose life was about to end. A single tear streamed down his cheek as he turned his head and slowly squeezed the trigger.

A blast of cold steel lightning blazed from the harpoon gun. There was a sickening thud and a sharp cry of pain as a black and white blur streaked with red flashed in front of Toby's horrified eyes. It took a moment for him to regain his senses and see what had happened. Murdo had hurled himself in the line of fire. He lay still and stiff in the water.

Toby, Serena, Maestro Baleeni, and the killer whales

swam to Murdo. They felt no breath, no heartbeat. Sealife and humans gathered around and through their grief they began to sing a requiem for a whale, they vowed, whose death would not be in vain. A song as sad as any could be was borne from the chorus, a song of compassion that would not be denied.

The whalemen tried to shut their ears. They tried to close their hearts. They fought back their tears, for whalemen were not supposed to cry. But this time the whalemen were no match for the music. One by one they began to surrender—singing softly at first so the others would not hear. When they heard their shipmates singing, the music grew louder and louder, spreading from man to man, ship to ship.

"BACK TO YOUR STATIONS! STOP THAT SINGING! THIS IS MUTINY!" The Dream Eater ranted and raved, but no one listened; no one even heard him.

Then, little by little, Nature's remedy, music, began to work its magic on the Dream Eater. As cold, as callous, as ruthless as Diomeda had become, there remained at the core of his being a place where love and compassion still resided. When the music reached that tiny chamber, it resonated there, and it was not long before his heart, his entire being, was taken over by the song.

Healed of his hatred, his insanity, his desire to be something he was not, Diomeda was free to return to the Stream of Dreams where he would be welcomed and dearly needed.

In a voice only Toby could hear he whispered: "Thank you Dream Singer. Now I understand."

And with that he drifted up and away.

The crusty captain of the fleet woke up bewildered. The old salt had lost his dreams long ago. The only songs that had ever moved him were gruffly sung whaling dirges. His skin was thick, but even he could not resist the sounds of Nature's symphony. He surrendered and sang of the feelings he had hidden so deep, so long. The whalemen, a rugged, hearty crew, laughed when they heard their captain singing like a sentimental old fool, but it was a good-natured laugh without malice or scorn.

With no one to give orders or to take them, *Nightmare* and the fleet of Iron Beasts slowed and finally shuddered to a full stop.

The battle had ended.

A song of victory, joy, and relief rose from the chorus to the heavens. Then, as if in answer, Nature performed a miracle. Murdo began to stir—his tail twitched; one eye opened, then the other. Slowly, Murdo began to swim. The harpoon had missed his vital organs. His right flipper was pierced clean through and there was a gash along his side, but it was a shallow wound that would heal.

Murdo's friends crowded around him.

"That was the bravest thing I ever saw." "Me, too, boss; you're the greatest!" "The best!" "Don't come any better!" " A real killer!"

Murdo grinned his familiar lopsided grin and in a soft voice he said, "If you're lookin' for a hero, don't look at me. Hear that music? That's the star of the show over there ... the Prince of Whales."

No words could express Toby's feelings; no thoughts could encompass his wonder. The whalemen were abandoning their ships, climbing down rope ladders to the welcoming arms of the people in the small boats. His family was near him, and Serena would be with him always and forever. It was like a dream come true, the clamor of jubilant sounds, the singing and laughter, the happy noise of celebration.

A dream come true ...

23

It is another night and the waters are calm again. A smiling crescent moon beams an enchanted light that glistens on the surface like an endless diamond, bathing the night in a shimmering crystal mist. There is music in the sea, intense and tranquil. The Iron Beasts have drifted away. Abandoned shells, they linger as silent reminders that a song not sung is soon forgotten. Toby will not forget. And when he sings, others will remember.

"Toby, wake up."

The quiet voice came from another place.

"Wake up," it came again.

Toby sang on. If this was a dream, he hoped it would never end.

THE BEST IN FANTASY